SAM KILLS CHRISTMAS

Also by Thomas Ridgewell

Art is Dead

SAM KILLS CHRISTMAS

THOMAS RIDGEWELL

CO-WRITTEN BY EDDIE BOWLEY

ILLUSTRATED BY DORINA HERDEWIJN

SPHERE

First published in Great Britain in 2018 by Sphere

Book design: aimiepricedesign.co.uk

1 3 5 7 9 10 8 6 4 2

A CIP catalogue record for this book is available from the British Library.

ISBN 978-0-7515-6305-4

Printed in Italy

Sphere
An imprint of
Little, Brown Book Group
Carmelite House
50 Victoria Embankment
London EC4Y 0DZ

An Hachette UK Company
www.hachette.co.uk

www.littlebrown.co.uk

Settle down children, it's time for a story!
But parents be warned, it gets kind of gory . . .

In a land far away lived a child named Sam
Who liked running and jumping and strawberry jam.
But Sam was an odd one, to all this was clear,
For their Christmas wish was the same every year:

'I want to kill santa!' Sam said with a roar,
'When I find that **Fruitcake!** you bet he's done for.
I'll bash him and smash him and chop off his head'.
Yes, as you can see, Sam wanted him dead.

One year Sam put bear traps all over the roof
With landmines built-in to make Santa go POOF.
And last year the chimney was filled up with knives
'Yet somehow,' Sam grumbled, 'he always survives!'

But this was the year that Sam knew what to get:
A new rocket launcher off the internet!
Straight out of the sky Santa's sleigh will be blown
(Hey kids, please remember, don't try this at home).

’Twas the night before Christmas, Sam jumped up and down
Because they knew that Santa was coming to town.
'This is the year Santa Claus will expire!'
A bleep on the radar? Well, 'Ready! Aim! FIRE!'

The BOOM that came after lit up the night sky
Both reindeer and presents rained down from on high
Sam ran to the crash site to witness the carnage
But what they found there was nothing but garbage.

'A robot! A fake!' It was all just a trick!
Sam had been fooled by a decoy Saint Nick.
But maybe this scrap and what's left of the sleigh
Could help Sam build something to chase down their prey?

The super-speed holly-copter powered by coal
Took to the skies headed towards the North Pole.
But before Sam could even get halfway from home
They had a strange feeling they were not alone.

It's Tinsel and Bauble, the jet-packing elves!

'You'll never reach Santa, we'll stop you ourselves!
We'll make you die hard and we'll do it with glee
You're about to be lit up like a Christmas tree!'

Sam steered into Bauble and chopped him in two
And out came his guts, made of glitter and glue.
'You turkey!' yelled Tinsel 'You murdered my bro!'
She locked on to Sam and launched her Missile-Toe.

PEW! WHOOSH! and ZOOM! The holly-copter went BOOM!

Sam leapt from the flames to avoid certain doom.

Then grabbed onto Tinsel and gave her a thwack

'Oi, Elf,' Sam demanded, 'Give me your jet-pack!'

Sam stayed in the air thanks to Tinsel's "donation"
On to the North Pole and their festive location.
When finally Sam saw a sight they knew well
'The Grotto! Now let's blow it to jingle bell!'

With the mightiest BLAM Sam kicked down the door

And charged right inside, armed and ready for war.

"Hey Santa, you **Cracker!**, I'm inside your house!"

But not a creature was stirring, not even a mouse.

Icicles formed and the door frame was blocked
The room soon froze over but Sam was not shocked.
They stood firm by the fireplace, refusing to flee
'I know who you are so come out and face me!'

Mist cleared to reveal the spine-chilling Ice Queen
'My my, what a horrible child you have been.'
She magically summoned an ice sword and said
'Let's see what you look like without that big head.'

The Queen swung her sword but it smashed when she missed.
Her teeth all fell out when her face met Sam's fist.
But pinned to the wall with an icicle dart
Sam was trapped as the Queen went straight for their heart.

Though stabbed in the chest, Sam's eyes simply rolled
For our hero's heart was already ice cold.
'Oh Frost!' the Queen whimpered as fear crossed her face
Before Sam shoved her into the hot fireplace.

While melting alive, she made one guarantee

'You'll never find the underground factory!'

The Ice Queen was soon just a puddle of water

And Sam knew where next to continue the slaughter.

Sam grabbed an axe and then walloped the floor
Until the ground broke when it could take no more.
Down into darkness Sam tumbled and fell
Hoping this was the place where old Santa would dwell.

Sam landed, SMASH! But in a turn of events
They'd fallen on top of a sack of presents.
A massive toy workshop! 'This must be the place!'
But there was no sign of life, not even a trace.

With a whip and a crack, Sam suddenly froze
The elves had thrown Christmas lights from the shadows
Then out of the darkness, a mighty voice boomed
'You shouldn't have come, child. Now you are doomed.'

Santa marched forward with a huge candy cane
Just the sight of that monster drove Sam quite insane.
'I'll kill you, you eggnog! It's gonna be violent!'
As Sam's voice rang out, the whole factory fell silent.

'Ho! Ho! Ho! Violence? Well, if you insist!
I'll just have to strike you off my naughty list.'
A laser gun sprang out of Kris Kringle's staff
'Just like Christmas crackers, I'll tear you in half!'

Things weren't looking good and Sam had to think quick
They used all their might as the trigger went CLICK
Sam yanked on the Christmas light whips hard and fast
Throwing all of the elves right in front of the blast.

The elves all exploded with a high-pitched 'Oh no!'
Their glittery elf guts fell down just like snow.
While Santa plucked body parts out of his beard
He suddenly realised, Sam had disappeared . . .

'You killed my parents!' Sam cried out with hatred.
'You clogged up the chimney and they suffocated.
It's your fault, you **yule log!** so what do you say
To the child whose family you took away?'

Santa thought for a moment but then said with cheer
'Oh, so what? That happens a few times a year!
It's simply a blunder, an easy mistake
So your parents died, don't be such a snowflake!'

But just then a light lasso caught Santa's foot
And wrapped 'round his legs so he had to stay put.
Sam strapped up the jet-pack and then waved bye-bye
As Santa Claus rocketed into the sky.

Sam loaded their axe in the candy-cane gun
And aimed to the sky, to avenge dad and mum.
'It looks like my wish is about to come true'
They fired the cannon and up the axe flew.

The rocket-pack burst with a mighty explosion
And Santa fell down in what felt like slow motion.
But he came to a stop before hitting the ground
It's atop the North Pole where his bones can be found.

Taking a seat upon Kris Kringle's throne
Sam took the name Santa in place of their own.
They spoke to the elves and made one thing quite clear
Christmas would work differently after this year.

No more naughty lists or poor parents departed
So that no other child would grow up cold hearted.
From now on they'd make sure to do all things right
Merry Christmas to all, and to all a good night.

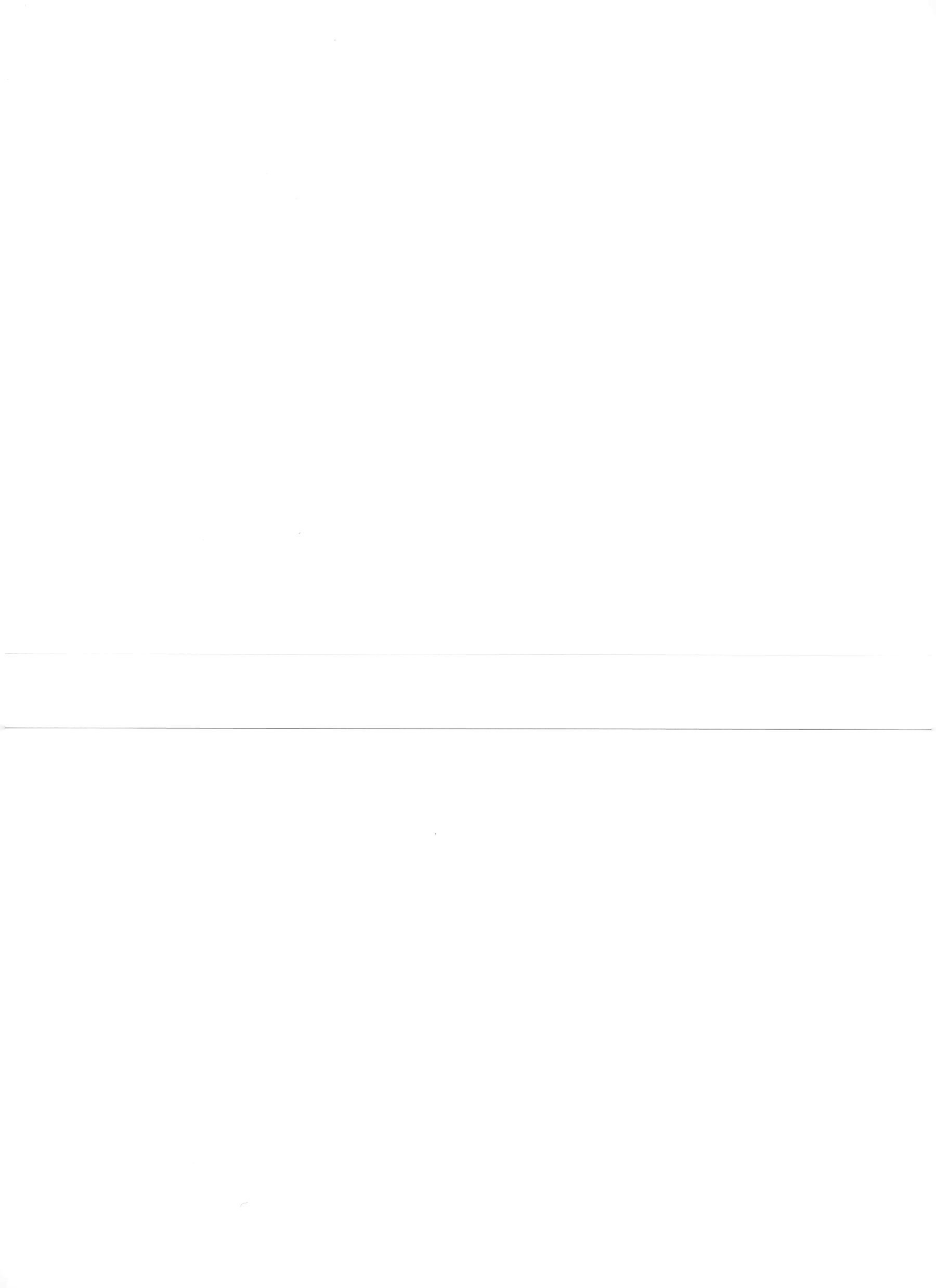

The End

THOMAS 'TOMSKA' RIDGEWELL is director, writer, and festivity fighter. He'd like to thank all the friends and loved ones who tried to show him the true meaning of Christmas; may they rest in peace. @thetomska

EDDIE BOWLEY (who actually really likes Christmas) is a freelance writer who's been working with Tom since 2013. Eddie would like to dedicate this to his totally real wife Alison and definitely human son Rik. @eddache_

DORINA HERDEWIJN is a freelancer with a bachelors degree in animation who enjoys painting, drawing and making cartoons. She'd like to thank her parents and that one teacher who called her an idiot. @dorinah_draws